W9-BOC-928

The Stolen Apples

Sigrid Heuck

Hart Publishing Company, Inc. • New York City

ISBN NO. 08055-1231-4
LIBRARY OF CONGRESS CATALOG CARD NO. 78-54176

MANUFACTURED IN THE UNITED STATES OF AMERICA

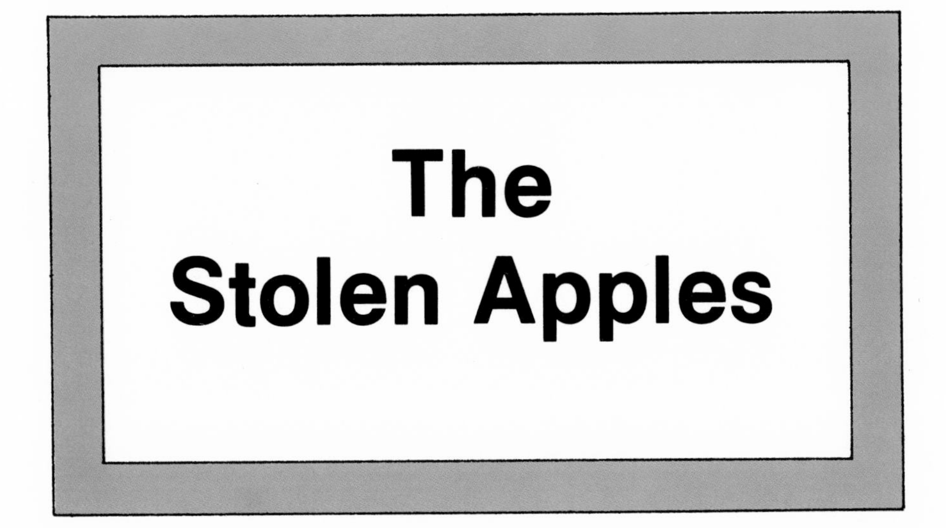

The Stolen Apples

This is a

A  and another 

and still more 

make a

Deep in the is a
In the is a
Behind the grows
an . Here, there lives
a .

At the end of every summer the

fall from the and the

fall in the Then the

eats so many his stomach

becomes as fat as a

One fine September morning the

had vanished. Not a single hung on the . Now each and every was bare. Not a single lay in the . The was very sad. Then he suddenly realized don't just run away, and he decided to find out who had taken them.

'Goodbye, !' he said.

'Goodbye, !' Off trotted the . In the he met a . 'Do you know who stole my ?' asked the .

'It wasn't me,' answered the .

'I don't like . But this morning something flew over my head. It might have been the thief.'

'Thank you,' said the .

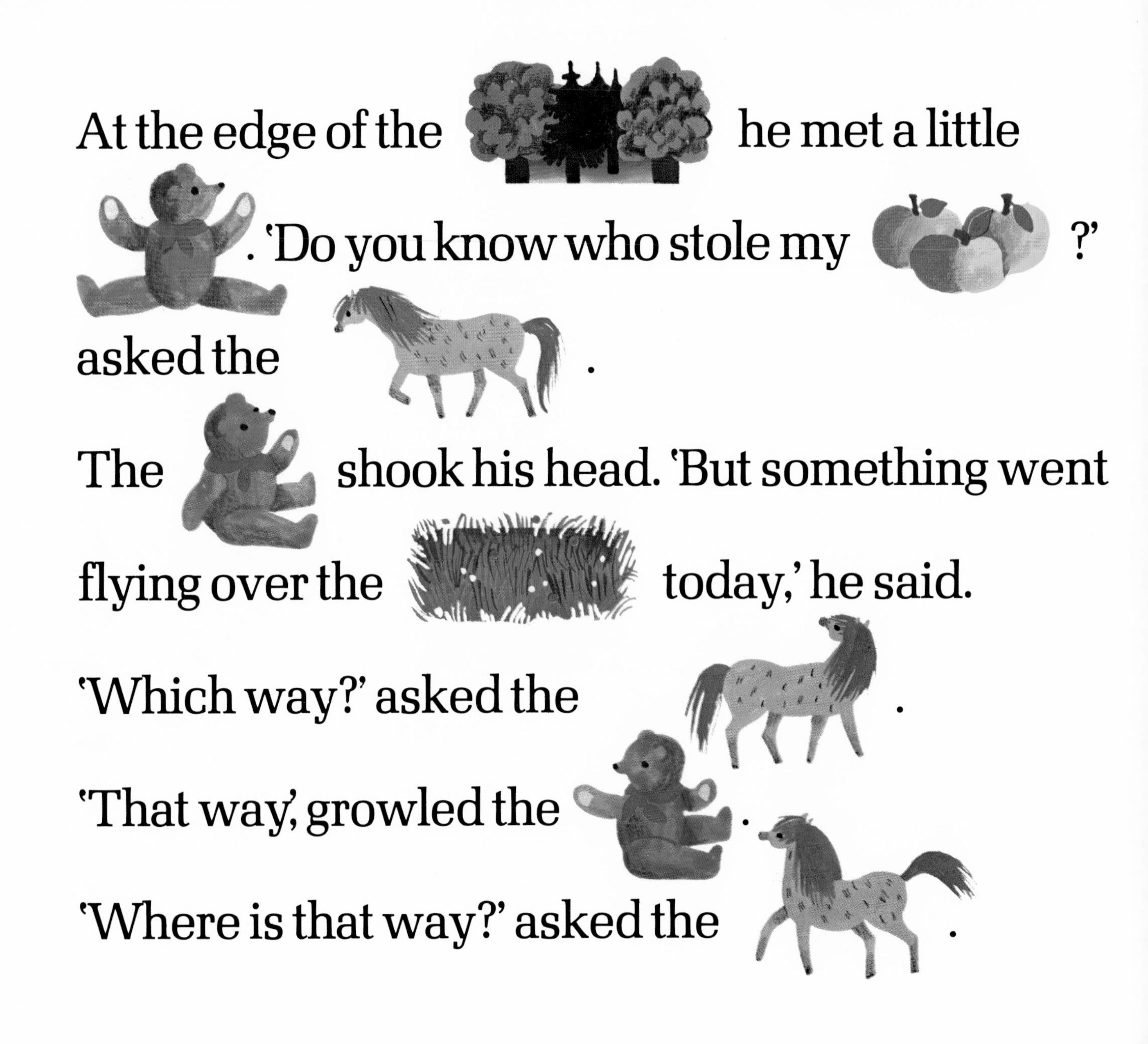

At the edge of the he met a little . 'Do you know who stole my ?' asked the .

The shook his head. 'But something went flying over the today,' he said.

'Which way?' asked the .

'That way,' growled the .

'Where is that way?' asked the .

'If I can ride on your back I'll show you!'
said the . Then the
with the on his back jumped over a
and splashed through a .
They passed some and a
and met a , ,
, ,
and
.

When the didn't know which way to go he stopped and asked: 'Now where?'

'That way,' the growled, pointing.

All of a sudden they had to stop. There in front of them was the

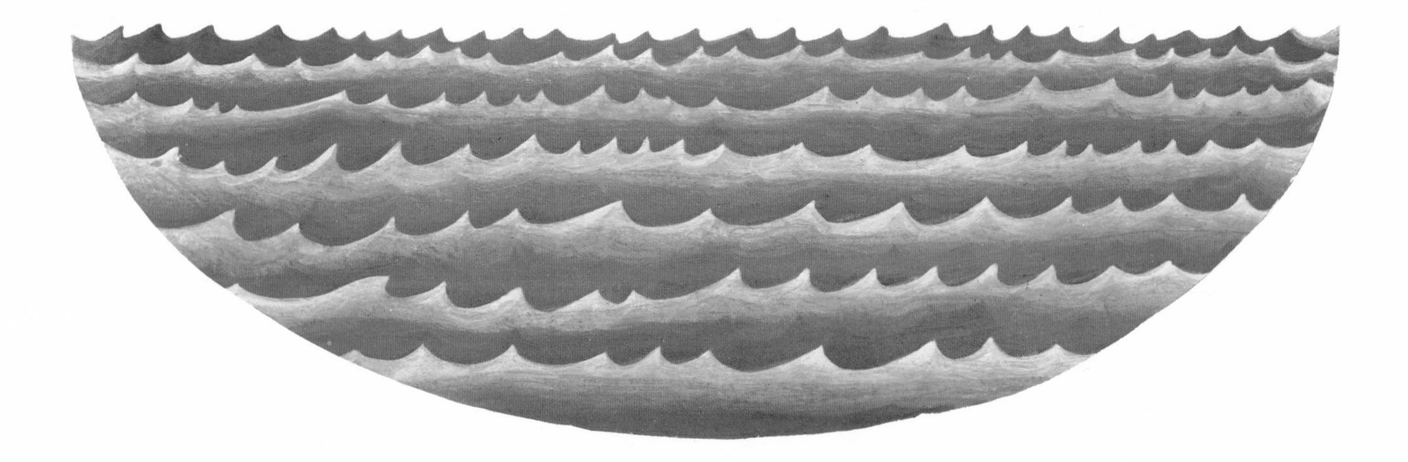

'We shall need a to take
us across the ,' said the
. They soon found a .
'We are looking for stolen
,' the told the .
'We have to cross the . If you will
take us, we'll give you an
on the way back,' promised the .

'One is not enough for my ,' said the .
'Then each of them shall have an ,' agreed the . 'I hope there's enough for everyone', muttered the . The accepted their offer and took them in his across the .

Sometime later they came to a land where the shone nearly all the time. They met an . 'Do you know who stole my ?' asked the when he saw the . 'Something flew over,' answered the .

'It wasn't the  . It wasn't the

. Perhaps it was .

They were carrying something. Ask the

. He always knows everything.'

The thanked him and promised

him an as a reward.

They looked for the and found
him at last. 'Have you seen my ?'
the asked him. 'Ah, that's
why the .
were making a noise', screeched the .
'Where can we find the ?'
asked the . Then the
took them to a . On every
sat a and each
had an in his beak.

The saw the and and croaked in fright. But because a cannot croak without opening his beak, the came tumbling down. The quickly gathered them up. 'Thank you for your help,' said the to the and gave him an as a reward.

Then the and the set off
for home again. As promised they gave the
an and one each to the
and his
. They trotted past the
and saw that they
had laid . The
had gone home and the
were
snuffling in their .

The ran after them.

They saw the being milked.

The had had a bath.

He was going to rest on the in

front of his .The went down

and it was dark in the .The

could not be seen. 'Anyway he

doesn't care about ,' said the

. 'Just as well,' growled the .

When at last they reached the in the deep in the they had only left, one for the and one for the . They had given all the rest away.

'It doesn't matter,' said the .'Next year when the  fall from the there will be many more. Then you will come and see me and we'll eat  until our stomachs are as fat as : 'Good,' said the 'see you next year!'

THE STOLEN APPLES

A Read-Together Rebus Story for Parent and Child

What child does not love to participate in the telling of a story? This book is specifically designed to involve the child in the story-reading session.

In practically every line, one or more words have been replaced with pictures—pictures that are easily identified and named by the child. Thus, parent and child share in the reading. The parent reads the printed words, and the child completes the thought by naming the picture for the missing word. The joy of achievement becomes a shared experience.

And the story itself is a sheer delight. Pictures and words are blended in perfect harmony to create a magical world. As pony and bear go in search of the stolen apples, the line between the real and the fanciful is sufficiently blurred to give the imagination free reign, and render the ordinary extraordinary.

Reading with and to children serves many purposes. A child on the lap, with an open, shared book epitomizes the warmth of family contact. Added, is the pleasurable excitement of entering the world of literature with all its treasures.

A child raised on such experiences will cherish reading as a favored activity. A rebus story allows the child to actively participate in the reading process. Proceeding across the page, line by line, translating pictures into words, and words into ideas, fosters a love of reading and promotes reading readiness.

About the Author

Sigrid Heuck, the German author-illustrator of *The Stolen Apples,* began her career as a writer and illustrator of children's books at the ripe old age of seven. For a long time, she couldn't decide whether she wanted to be a farmer's wife or a bareback rider in the circus, but since she loved to draw, she eventually chose to study commercial art. Her first published book, written and illustrated by herself, received a silver medal in 1960. Since then, she has been turning out award-winning picture books and children's books, as well as illustrating the works of other authors.

For the setting for *The Stolen Apples* she did not have to go further than her own backyard, for Sigrid Heuck lives in a wooden house she herself built in the Alps, surrounded by a small forest, a meadow, five apple trees, three ponies, two dogs, and two swans.

Hart Publishing Company, Inc.
New York City